The **GREAT TRUCK RESCUE**

SIMON & SCHUSTER BOOKS FOR YOUNG READERS
An imprint of Simon & Schuster Children's Publishing Division
1230 Avenue of the Americas, New York, New York 10020
Copyright © 2008 by JRS Worldwide, LLC
TRUCKTOWN and JON SCIESZKA'S TRUCKTOWN and design are trademarks of JRS Worldwide, Inc.
All rights reserved, including the right of reproduction in whole or in part in any form.
SIMON & SCHUSTER BOOKS FOR YOUNG READERS is a trademark of Simon & Schuster, Inc.
For information about special discounts for bulk purchases, please contact Simon
& Schuster Special Sales at 1-866-506-1949 or business@simonandschuster.com.
The Simon & Schuster Speakers Bureau can bring authors to your live event. For
more information or to book an event, contact the Simon & Schuster Speakers
Bureau at 1-866-248-3049 or visit our website at www.simonspeakers.com.
Book design by Lucy Ruth Cummins
The text for this book is set in Truck King.
The illustrations for this book are digitally rendered.
Manufactured in China
0510 SCP
First Simon & Schuster Books for Young Readers paperback edition August 2010
2 4 6 8 10 9 7 5 3 1
Library of Congress Cataloging-in-Publication Data
Scieszka, Jon.
[Melvin might?]
The great truck rescue / Jon Scieszka ;
illustrated by David Shannon, Loren Long, David Gordon.
p. cm. – (Jon Scieszka's Trucktown)
Summary: Melvin, a cautious cement mixer, worries that he cannot keep up with the
other trucks, but when Rita needs help, he overcomes his fear in order to help her.
ISBN 978-1-4424-0932-3 (pbk. : alk. paper)
[1. Trucks–Fiction. 2. Worry–Fiction.] I. Shannon, David, 1959– ill. II. Long, Loren, ill.
III. Gordon, David, 1965 Jan. 22– ill. IV. Title.
PZ7.S41267Gr 2010
[E]–dc22 2010005361
Previously Published as Melvin Might? by Simon & Schuster Books for Young Readers

Characters and environments developed by the

David Shannon · Loren Long · David Gordon
ILLUSTRATION CREW

Drawings by
Juan Pablo Navas

Executive Producer

Color by
Isabel Nadal

in association with
ANIMAGIC S. L.

Creative Supervisor
Sergio Pablos

Art Director
Dan Potash

To Justin, because
he always tries
—J. S.

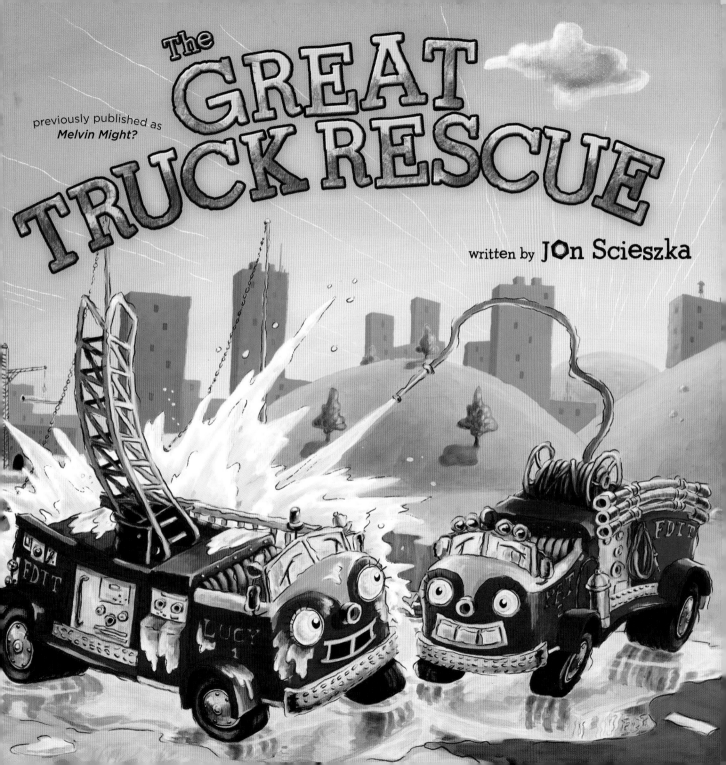

Cement Mixer Melvin worries.

Melvin worries, "I might get dirty."

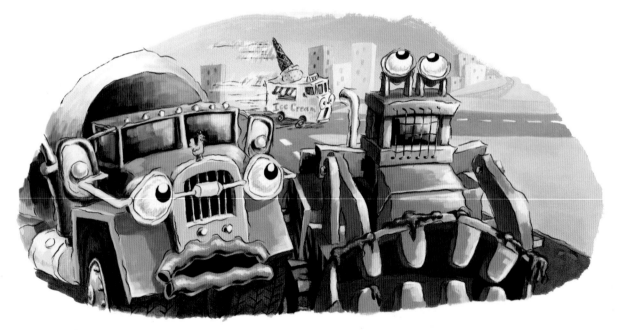

Melvin worries, "I might get stuck."

Melvin worries, "I might get *worried*."

"Wow," says Pete.
"You are making
ME worried."

"Come on, Melvin," says Jack. "The bridge isn't finished. But we found a great new way to get across."

This worries Melvin even more.

"First you
ROAR!"
says Pete.
Pete roars down the hill.

"Me too," beeps Rita. Rita roars down the hill.

"Oh no," says Melvin. "I can't try that."

"Then you **SOAR!**" yells Pete.

Pete soars through the air.

"Me too," beeps Rita.
Rita soars through the air.

"Oh no," says Melvin.
"I can't try that."

"Then you **SPLASH!**" says Pete.
Pete lands with a splash.

"Uh-oh," beeps Rita.
Rita doesn't quite splash.

Jack says, "Come on, Melvin. Follow me!"

"Oh no," worries Melvin.
"I can't try any of that."

beeps Rita.

"Yes, I need help," says Melvin.

"HELP!
HELP!"
beeps Rita.

Melvin sees that Rita really
needs help.

But Jack and Pete are gone.

"But I'm worried I can't."

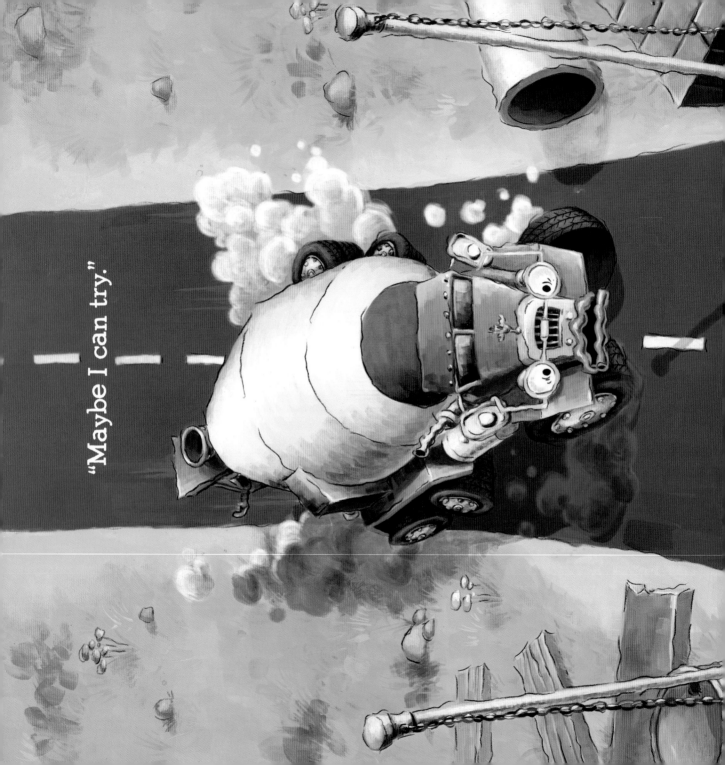

Melvin **ROARS** down the hill.

"Maybe I can try."

Melvin **SOARS** through the air.

But he gives Rita a push.

"I can try."

"I can try."

Melvin saves Rita with one big ...

Jack and Pete come racing back.
"Melvin!" honks Pete. "You did it!"

"You roared! You soared!
You really splashed!"
says Jack.

"I know," says Melvin . . .

"...but I think I might still worry."

"Me too," beeps Rita.

And Rita and Melvin
slowly drive home.